Bouncing Time

by patricia hubbell
pictures by melissa sweet

HarperCollins Publishers

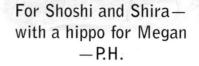

For Shoshi and Shira—
with a hippo for Megan
—P.H.

To Amelia
—M.S.

Bouncing Time
Text copyright © 2000 by Patricia Hubbell
Illustrations copyright © 2000 by Melissa Sweet

Printed in Singapore at Tien Wah Press.

http://www.harperchildrens.com

Library of Congress Cataloging-in-Publication Data
Hubbell, Patricia.
Bouncing time / by Patricia Hubbell; illustrated by Melissa Sweet.
p. cm.
Summary: An exuberant infant bounces through the day's activities,
including a trip to the zoo.
ISBN 0-688-17376-4 (trade)—ISBN 0-688-17377-2 (library)
[1. Babies Fiction.   2. Parent and child Fiction.   3. Stories in rhyme.]
I. Sweet, Melissa, ill.   II. Title.   PZ8.3.H848Bo 2000
[E]—dc21   99-15501   CIP

1 2 3 4 5 6 7 8 9 10
❖
First Edition

How will you **bounce** today, baby?

BOUNCE!

BOUNCE!

BOUNCE!

Will you **bounce** like a grasshopper, cricket, or frog?

Or a hoppity toad
on his log in the bog?

Will you **bounce** like your clown
doing tricks on his mat?

Like your bouncy-bounce puppy?
Like your pouncy-pounce cat?

Come climb in your backpack.
We'll **bounce** to the zoo.
You'll peek from your pouch
like a young kangaroo.

We'll see tigers that tumble,

and jumping giraffes,

and a big bouncy lion

making everyone laugh.

Monkeys will somersault.
Pythons will flip.

Cuddly old panda
will hop, jump, and skip.

Hippo will **bounce**.
Elephant, too.

Oh, the whole zoo will **bounce**
when they see bouncing you!

Then we'll wave a good-bye
to the bouncity zoo.
We'll **bounce** our way home.

Bouncy me!
Bouncy you!

And after your supper
and bath are all through,
you'll **bounce** into bed—

and I'll bounce in, too.

The stars and the moon
will glitter and gleam
as you dream of the
wonderful things
you have seen.

Good night, bouncy one.